THREE BROTHER BEARS

BEARS

Stephen Grant
ILLUSTRATED BY JILL HARDIN

AuthorHouse™
1663 Liberty Drive
Bloomington, IN 47403
www.authorhouse.com
Phone: 1 (800) 839-8640

Because of the dynamic nature of the Internet, any web addresses or links contained in this book may have changed
since publication and may no longer be valid. The views expressed in this work are solely those of the author and do
not necessarily reflect the views of the publisher, and the publisher hereby disclaims any responsibility for them.

Any people depicted in stock imagery provided by Getty Images are models,
and such images are being used for illustrative purposes only.
Certain stock imagery © Getty Images.

This book is printed on acid-free paper.

ISBN: 978-1-7283-3530-8 (sc)
ISBN: 978-1-7283-3529-2 (e)

Print information available on the last page.

Published by AuthorHouse 04/01/2020

authorHOUSE®

MOTHER IS WATCHING

Once three bear brothers were wrestling in the field, pouncing on each other and proving who was strongest. Just then a deer wandered out of the woods. The brothers stopped and watched the deer. The oldest said, "You go left, I'll go right, and you can go up the middle and we will get the deer." And so they did. The youngest bear stalked to the right, the oldest to the left, and the middle age bear stalked straight toward the deer. As they quietly approached, they became excited and they all charged. The deer heard them and at the last moment jumped! The brothers ran into each other... knocking their heads together! They fell back in the grass and shook their heads as the deer walked away. Their mother, watching the whole thing said, "Ridiculous!"

The next day, the three bear brothers found a creek. They followed the creek to the rapids and saw fish jumping in the air. The fish were shiny and silver and jumped so high. The water was moving fast and the brothers were at first unsure if they should go in. The fish were so close and they couldn't help themselves. They charged toward the fish. They jumped for the closest fish and knocked heads and fell back into the water! The fish swam away and the mother said, "Silly boys!"

That night, the bear brothers decided they would catch something to eat this time and nothing would stop them. The oldest said, you go to the bottom of the ravine. We will heard the deer to the edge and they will fall to you and we will eat our fill. The two bears stalked quietly toward the deer. The deer stepped back, closer and closer to the cliff. The bears became excited and charged once again! The deer leapt into the air. The bear knocked heads and fell of the cliff and on top of their brother below.

Ouch they said. Their mother, watching, said, "Oh my goodness" and ran to them. When she reached her sons, the bear brothers couldn't stop laughing. They were rolling around on the ground with laughter. In fact they laughed all the way home.

Daddy Wants a Nap

Daddy bear was laying down in the den to begin his afternoon nap. Mother was there too. The boys were not sleeping, though. First the youngest bear came in and snuggled between mom and dad. His head in mothers back and his feet in daddy's back, he wriggled and squiggled and woke everyone up! "What are you doing?" said daddy bear. "I'm snuggling" said youngest bear. "Get back to your bed!" bellowed daddy bear and go to sleep. After a while, a dozen squirrels ran through the den and right over daddy and mother bear! "What was that?" asked mother bear. "It's those darn squirrels again" replied daddy bear. He got up and chased them out. Soon afterwards, the middle son sneaked into the parents den and slid between mother and father. He kicked and he twitched and he rolled about. Daddy bear rolled over, "Grrooowwwll, get out of our bed!" Mother said, Shhhhhh" and middle age bear cried and ran out of the den. "Awwwww", said daddy bear. Mother and Father lumbered into the baby bear den and found their boys huddled, awake and crying. They said, "We want to play!" Mother and Father sat between them and they hugged and snuggled and fell asleep together.

HOW COULD WE HUNT?

Three baby bears were walking behind their father during their first hunt. Their father, an old grizzly bear, has many years of hunting experience. The baby bears were nervous about hunting and kept whimpering as they followed. It was a long way to the hunting grounds on the edge of the mountain. Bear cubs don't like heights. The oldest brother was brave and said, "Don't worry, just stay next to me." Daddy sat down with them once they reached the mountain peak. "Look below us boys," he said. "There are thousands of deer, rabbits, squirrels, and foxes all for us. All you need to do is have the courage to try. Don't worry about missing and making a mistake." The youngest bear asked his father, "Have you ever missed a deer?" Father bear said, "Of course I have missed many deer." The boys looked surprised. The oldest said, "But daddy, you always bring home dinner!" The middle aged bear shook his head in agreement. Father saw that he must do more than talk to the boys to get them to try catching their first deer. "Boys," he said, "I see that you need more than encouragement, so I am going to leave you here. You will get hungry and soon you will realize that you must hunt if you want to survive. Then you will learn more quickly how to hunt." All three bears moaned and cried "No father, don't leave us!" It was too late. Their dear father bear lumbered down the peak toward home, leaving the bears.

They couldn't believe what had happened. After talking about it, they realized there was only one thing to do. Find some prey. The oldest was a good tracker and quickly found a trail to follow. Rabbits were drinking water at the local stream. The youngest pounced and missed. The middle age bear caught the smallest rabbit by the tail.

The oldest bear swatted the oldest rabbit with his paw and caught him! Two rabbits ... what luck on their first hunt. Their father, watching from far away was very proud of his boys.

Next, the three brothers cornered some squirrels in a tree. The youngest climbed up and knocked the squirrels out of the branches. They fell directly into his brothers paws.

Their first hunting expedition was a success! Father bear walked back into view and asked them, "So, are you hungry? Did you catch any prey?" The boys looked at each other and smiled and said, "Father, we could only catch a few grubs. Can you find dinner for us?" Father, knowing they were lying, realized they just wanted to watch their father in action one more time. Smiling, he said, "Watch this." He bounded down the mountain toward a large moose and leapt onto its back! The boys gasped and cried out, "Father! Don't hurt yourself!" But the moose had no chance since he was surprised. They looked in awe and he gave each of them the best parts of the moose. They said, "Father, we already killed and ate our fill. We just wanted to watch you again."

Father chuckled and pounced on them, almost tickling them to death! "It's okay boys," he said. "Your dad likes to show off sometimes." They all came home very proud to be a part of their family. Knowing that bravery is a part of their tradition.

DANGER!

Mother and father bear were out of the den hunting one morning. The three brother bears were sleeping in late when the youngest woke in fear. "I ... I hear something," he stuttered. They listened and heard a low growl and soft paws trampling the leaves. It was Tigra the mountain lion! The bears huddled together in their den listening. The oldest said, "Let's run out of the den and fight him!" The youngest shook his head no. The middle age bear agreed they should stay there. Just then Tigra roared and bellowed and shook his tail. He was trying to make them run out. The oldest said, "Come on, we can take him." The youngest said, "I'm staying here." The middle bear said, "He's too big for us."

The lion roared again, because he could smell them and even hear them. Out of the trees came father bear!

Bounding and charging, he knocked Tigra off his paws. Mother bear came behind and bellowed out. Tigra saw he was out numbered and retreated to the forest. The brother bears came running out of the den crying. Mother bear caught them. The middle aged bear asked, "Where have you been?" Father Bear said, "You were never in danger, we were just across the ravine hunting when we heard Tigra roar." The boys ran to father and tackled him in the gut as father went ooof! The wrestled with father and jumped on his stomach. Father called out, "Mother, do you have some Advil?"

THE SHOWDOWN

The oldest bear brother was still angry about the incident with Tigra the day before. He went to his father, "I want to go and fight Tigra," he said. Father bear knew that his son's bravery was something he should support, but how could he keep his son safe while allowing him to fight an adult mountain lion! "Come with me," he said. They walked together through the forest. The son realized they were getting close to Tigra's den and he started to get nervous. His father noticed and did his best to calm his oldest son. "Don't worry, I will be there and you won't get hurt," he said. The son wasn't so sure. When they walked into the clearing in front of Tigra's den they only saw one lion cub playing nearby. He was the oldest of Tigra's sons and a fierce fighter. Father bear pushed his son toward Tigra's son and convinced him this is the mountain lion he should fight.

The son liked his chances and boldly charged the mountain lion with mouth open wide. The mountain lion snarled and ducked the charge, swiping his claws at the bear.

As they circled each other, Tigra emerged from the den and locked eyes with Father Bear. He snarled, but didn't move; knowing that this is not his fight.

Oldest bear leapt at oldest lion. The dust grew and covered them. Nothing could be seen except tails and blurry fur. Then a growl and snarl came from the mess and both fell backwards. It was a tie! The oldest bear walked back to his father. "I'm done," and they decided to head home. Tigra congratulated his son for standing his ground. Father bear congratulated his son for facing his fears as they returned home.

THE BEAR BACK RIDE

Father Bear was returning from his afternoon bath in the river. As he walked the water dripped off his fur. He shook his whole body and water flew everywhere. Just then, youngest bear ran to him saying, "Father, can I get on your shoulders?" Father Bear said, "I suppose so, but I am wet and you might slip off." Youngest Bear jumped up as Father Bear laid in the dirt. "Aww, I just took a bath and I'm already getting dirty, "said Father Bear. Youngest Bear didn't care as he scrambled up to Fathers shoulders. He could see much farther when Father stood on his back legs. He saw his brothers bounding toward them as the cried, "We want to ride on your back too! Pleeeassse?" Father crouched down and laid in the dirt again while Middle Aged Bear and Oldest Bear climbed onto Father's back. "Go Daddy Go! So Father Bear jumped up and moved to the left and then he moved to the right and all the brothers were tossed around yelling and screaming, "Yeah Daddy!" The brothers were close together and started bonking heads and wrestling. Father Bear growled, "Stop that." Too late though, because Middle aged bear started slipping off Father Bear's wet back. He was holding onto youngest brother's leg and Father's belly fur while trying not to fall. Father Bear looked underneath his belly and asked, "What are you doing down there?" Middle Aged Bear was not happy since he was bouncing between the ground and Father's belly. "Ooof! Said Middle Bear while bouncing around. His brothers were laughing at him when Middle aged Bear decided to stop this mess. He punched Father Bear in the Gut and Father said, "Ooof, stop that!" and Father rolled over on his side. The brothers were launched in the air and landed in a bush laughing. Middle Bear gasped for breathe and Father Bear was saying, "Mother, get me some Advil!"

BUTTERFLIES AND FAMILY

It turns out that bear brothers love butterflies. The youngest brother bear especially loves to chase them through the glen.

Pouncing, reeling, dancing, and prancing, the brother bears chase after the butterflies. Mother watches and sees a problem. "You are supposed to be hunting deer today," she exclaimed, but the brothers were not listening. They were not watching either because behind them at the tree line were two does and one buck. They were eating the grass and watching the bears. Mother said, "Ridiculous!" as she laid down in the grass in disgust. Youngest brother caught a butterfly between his lips and walked over to mother. "Look what I have!" he said. Mother said, "It's a beautiful butterfly dear." "Can I keep it?" asked youngest bear? "No, you should let the butterfly live its life and fly free," replied the mother. Youngest brother thought that was an excellent idea and let the butterfly go. Mother stomped off to make lunch for her boys. When she was ready she called youngest bear. "Dear, I need you to bring your brothers to the den for lunch," she said. Youngest bear was excited and said "Okay!" Then he jumped out of the den and yelled, "Its lunch time...come and get it!"

Mother spun about and said, "Hey! That's too loud. I think all of Denver could hear you." "Momma, what's Denver?" youngest bear asked. Mother just sighed and served the boys their venison and water.

TRUST

The three bear brothers were playing down by the brook one day. They enjoyed swimming and splashing and tackling each other. The youngest loved to jump off the tall rock and make big splashes. The middle age bear was always splashing water and running through the shallow places. The oldest liked to swim under the water and look for fish and turtles.

The oldest was under water when the youngest did a belly flop on top of him! Their middle brother just happened to be running through the water and slipped and fell into both of his brothers! "Ooowwa," they all said because they bonked each other's heads...again. The oldest brother swallowed some water wrong, though, and he was coughing. The other two were scared for him and asked him what should they do? The oldest acted like he wanted mother and father. His younger brothers knew the way back to the den so they ran fast through the water and disappeared into the trees. The oldest hoped they understood what he meant as he laid down on a warm rock.

The younger brothers tripped here and fell there as they bounded through the forest. Finally, they reached the den, but their parents were not there.

The older brother was waiting and wondered how long would it take for his brothers to get back to the den. Should he try to move? No. He will wait because he knows his brothers won't let him down.

The young bears cried out and their parents came around the corner of the rocky outcropping. What is it dear, said mother bear? Older Brother is hurt because he swallowed too much water! Their parents charged toward the brook with the most speed. When they arrived they found their oldest laying on a boulder in the sun. He sat up and greeted them, but then pain came across his face. He was safe, but no more swimming for a while. Oldest brother thanked his brothers for finding their parents and keeping him safe.

BERRY HUNTING

The three brother bears were walking through the woods one day when they decided to look for berries. The youngest brother went left, the oldest bear went right, and the middle bear walked straight. They were looking for berries for what seemed like an hour, but one called out I found berries. The middle bear and the oldest bear ran back to the center, but were careful not to bonk heads. They said, "where's younger brother?!" They called out, "Hey brother where are you!" No one answered. Actually youngest brother bear had found berries and could hear his brothers, but decided not to answer. He wanted the berries for himself. In fact his face was purple already with berry juice. The other brothers came bounding through the forest looking for him and ran straight into the youngest bear and the berry bush and they bonked heads.

Ugh, not again! Oldest brother said, "Hey! Why didn't you tell us you found berries?!" Middle brother gave his younger brother two punches in the shoulder and said, "Yeah!" Youngest brother punched oldest brother in the gut and then they all started fighting and wrestling and howling. Mother and Father came over to see what was happening. They were caught up in the wrestling and all of them rolled into the berry patch.

They were covered in berries and juice from the paws to their face and all though their hair. Father growled, "Stop!" Mother said, "You clean them up and stomped off toward the Den." Father Bear growled to the boys, "You're in big trouble now!" The boys started laughing until father picked them up by the scruff of their neck and dragged them to the river. Father Bear scrubbed and dunked and scrubbed and dunked until the brothers were drenched and clean of all the berries. The lumbered back to the Den where Father found mother in her water hole. He saw some berry still on her nose and said, "Dear, there's some berry left on your nose." Mother said, "Why don't you come over here and lick it off?" The boys, hiding behind Father laughed and said, "Ewww!" And laughed as they ran away from Father and his big old growl.

MOTHER BEAR SAVES THE DAY

The brother bears were having an argument, one morning, over who would be the first to go swimming and who was the best swimmer. The middle bear said he was the best swimmer, the oldest brother said he was stupid and didn't know anything. They pushed and shoved and wrestled each other. Youngest brother started crying and said stop fighting it hurts my ears. Mother walked into the Den and announced, "We are going on an adventure!" The brothers looked at each other like, did you know about this? Youngest bear said, "But momma aren't we going swimming today?" "No sir!" said mother bear. I have something special planned for each of you. Anger turned to excitement in the brothers eyes. Questions of where and when and what flew at mother bear like a flock of seagulls hunting for fish. Mother bear stood there and smiled as the brothers pawed at her for information. "Finally, mother bear said, it's a secret but I promise you will all enjoy it." The brothers knew what that meant. No more questions, mother had put her paw down. After breakfast, mother bear led her boy cubs on a trek through the woods. They passed the glen and the river. They passed the hunting grounds and the Tiger den. They were in a new part of the woods they had never been before. Mother knew that oldest brother enjoyed learning about human things, so they stopped at an old rusted car near a cliff. "Look and then tell me what happened," she said to her oldest. Oldest brother saw the big bend in the car. He saw the blackness on the inside. He pointed at the empty inside and said, "Someone made a mistake the car fell from up there and it had a fire," he said. "Very good," mother said. "You are a very smart bear." Oldest brother's chest puffed out and his brothers looked on him with big eyes. Next mother bear asked middle age bear to stalk a fox on the far side of a glen. Middle bear quietly approached the fox, getting very close, until a twig snapped. The fox jumped and ran.

Middle bear followed close behind. They ran left, and right. They ran between trees and under bushes. The fox was getting tired and slowed down. Middle bear caught up to fox, but stopped and pranced back to mother bear. He said, "Mother, I caught the fox, but let it go since I'm not hungry." Mother bear praised her son and the brothers looked at him with awe and admiration. The mother bear asked youngest brother to climb a tall tree and show us some acrobatics. Youngest bear chose the tallest tree and climbed up the tree trunk quickly. He swung from branch to branch and dangled from the largest branch by one paw! Then he scrambled down the trunk and walked confidently to mother bear. "You are so quick and I thought you were going to fall!" His brothers were amazed at youngest bear's acrobatics. Now it was mother's turn. Mother said, "Follow me, we are climbing that mountain." "Why?" asked her cubs. "I have something to show you that you will only see in the snow," she said as she led them up the steep mountain. Up and up they climbed. Above the trees they went. Higher and higher until all other mountains were below them. The youngest looked out and saw forever. The middle bear wondered if they'd ever find their way back to the den. The oldest brother bear was so excited to see something new and go somewhere he had never been. Mother stopped and stared. The bear brothers stopped too and looked. Mother whispered, "look over there...can you see the white bears?" The brothers squinted at the bright white snow and saw something moving. More than one thing. Was it three? "Yes, momma, yes...we see them!" Mother Bear quieted them down and said, "Those are polar bears...

We won't visit them today since father is not with us. I just wanted to show you something you had never seen before...that's my talent." They returned home by sliding down the mountain snow on their backs. Sometimes they rode on mother's back. Oldest brother slid into his younger brothers and they rolled and slide the rest of the way down the snowy part of the mountain. They walked all the way home past the forest, Tigre's den, the river and the glen. When they arrived at their Den, father bear asked, "Where have you been?" The brothers bears jumped on father bear, knocked him down and stepped laid on top of him while licking his face. "Whoa!" said father bear. "Oh, my guts, you got me!" he said. "Do you have any Advil?" father bear asked mother.

POLAR BEAR NEIGHBORS

Father and Mother were talking quietly. The brother bears heard them as they woke that morning. The brothers looked at each other. Either they were in trouble or something big was about to happen. They were worried and excited at the same time. Slowly and quietly they walked out of the den and sat near their parents. "Boys, remember the polar bear family?" asked Father Bear. The brothers nodded yes. "We are going to visit them today," said Father Bear. The brothers jumped and leaped and ran about for joy. They couldn't believe it! They asked so many questions, mother had to shush them. It was time to go and they had a long trek ahead of them. The brothers were tired of walking when they arrived at the mountain. The sight of snow excited them and they leapt and bounded up the mountain. Father growled when they reached the Polar bear den and the brothers knew to stop and wait. As mother watched over them, father bear walking quietly into the Polar Bear's clearing. The Father Polar Bear stood on his back feet and huffed and puffed as he saw the grizzly bear walk slowly into his clearing.

He approached father bear and the brothers were nervous. Father bear stopped and waited for the large white polar bear to approach him. They circled each other and sniffed. The mother and daughter polar bears came out of their den to watch. Father Polar Bear seemed to understand that this was a friendly visit. He looked back at his family and moaned a happy sound as if to say, come and meet our guests!

Father Bear did the same and the brother bears romped into the middle of all of them ... bonking heads and running into Father Polar bear too.

So embarrassing thought Father Bear, but the Polar Bear seemed to laugh and at the same time groan in pain. Youngest brother licked the Father Bear on his chest and ran to meet the young polar bear daughter. Middle Bear beat him to the den and introduced himself with a silly growl. He got a big paw in the face as the girl polar bear seemed playful as she ran towards the woods. What a wonderful day for both families!

THE ICE SKATING INCIDENT

One cold winter morning, the Grizzly Bear Family was sleeping in the den, enjoying their long winter's hibernation. The stream nearby had frozen over and the squirrel family was sliding and slipping on the ice. This is the time of year that Polar Bears come down from the mountain to search for food. The Polar Bear family lumbered through the forest and found the frozen stream with squirrels and other animals. The daughter polar bear jumped over the snow bank, making the squirrels run and hide. The squirrels ran to the Grizzly Bear Den and sat on top of the Den in the snow. The chattered about how many nuts to eat when the daughter polar bear found them again. Startled, they fell over the edge and into the den and on top of Father Bear! Father Bear woke up with snow and squirrels falling on him and growled, "What is this? A squirrel avalanche?"

The Brother bears woke up too and saw father swatting the squirrels off of his face. Mother said, "Shhhh, I'm trying to sleep." The squirrels ran out of the Den and into Father Polar Bear's legs. Father Grizzly looked out and saw his old friend and gave a warm and long grrrrr. Father Polar Bear was surprised and happy to find his friend, although he looked sleepy. Father Polar Bear invited Father Bear to come out and enjoy the ice. Father Bear called for his cubs, but they were already jumping and bounding through the snow toward the icy stream. Just then, oldest brother's eyes locked onto daughter polar bear's eyes. They sniffed the air and then chased each other into the woods. The younger brothers started laughing and the father's just shook their heads. Mother came out to scold everyone for being so loud when out of the woods sprang daughter Polar Bear and oldest brother. They slide into the younger brothers and then right into Father Bear's belly! "Oooof," said Father Bear as we double over with pain. "Honey....I need some Advil!" Growled out Father Bear.

Everyone was laughing...especially Father Polar Bear. Mother Polar Bear, watching the whole thing, said, "Ridiculous!" Mother Bear agreed.

FATHER RETURNS FROM A HUNT

Spring time had come and Father Bear had gone hunting. As the bear cubs started to wake, they realized how hungry they were. Mother Bear understood, "Boys, you should be hungry after sleeping all winter." The youngest brother didn't believe that he slept all winter..."Mother, we only slept one night! What are you talking about!!?" Mother pointed at his ruffled fur and how much taller he was. "See," she said, "You grew a whole paw taller and all of your fur is dirty." Then she tickled him and made him promise to believe in hibernation. "Mother, can we have something to eat?" asked middle aged bear. Mother took them out to the berry patch and they picked the last few berries.

Just then Father Bear returned. He had a sly look on his face. "I'm sorry everyone ... I just couldn't find any deer. The squirrels ran too fast. Even the foxes out foxed me." The oldest brother bear didn't believe him. He saw that look on Father's face before, "You've got something don't you." he said. "I see that look on your face!" The other brothers ran and jumped on Father Bear..."We're hungry!" Father Bear let it out, "Okay, I guess you can have some deer meat ... but not both of them!" Mother Bear gave Father Bear a big hug. "You caught two deer!"

The whole family eat all they could eat and then some more. It was a wonderful spring time and they decided to sing a song.

Youngest Bear started, "God our Father, God our Father, we thank you, we thank you, for our many blessing, for our many blessings, Amen, Amen."

GOOD NIGHT BEARS

Mother was putting oldest Brother Bear to bed when he asked for a story. Mother thought for a moment and said, "When I first met your Father, we went to a human baseball game. Your father enjoyed the game because the humans were playing together. He also didn't understand why the humans needed umpires and would argue with them. Father would say, 'Why do the humans argue with the umpires? They already know who is right and who is wrong." Mother said she knew Father was a good Bear right away. Just then, Father came in with the other two cubs and tucked them into their sleeping place. Middle aged bear wanted a story from Mother Bear too. Mother started a story how her brothers were very protective of her when she first met Father Bear. Her brothers would ask, "How do you know you are safe" and, "Shouldn't we check up on him?"

Mother looked at Father Bear ..."I said no I didn't need them to check up on Father Bear because he loves everyone no matter who they are. He has no enemies, and he forgives other bears who treat him badly." Father Bear's face got all red and said, "That's not fair, I didn't know you were going to embarrass me." The cubs saw their chance and they all jumped off their sleeping place onto Father Bear and they bonked their heads as the jam piled on top of him while laughing.

Printed in the United States
By Bookmasters